For Shelley
N.M.

For Annabel
A.A.

ORCHARD BOOKS
338 Euston Road
London NW1 3BH

Orchard Books Australia
Hachette Children's Books
Level 17/207 Kent Street, Sydney, NSW 2000

First published in 1995 by Orchard Books
First published in paperback 1996
This edition published in 2007

Text © Nicola Moon 1995
Illustrations © Alex Ayliffe 1995

A CIP catalogue record for this book is available from the British Library.

ISBN 978 1 84616 578 8

1 3 5 7 9 10 8 6 4 2
Printed in China

Orchard Books is a division of Hachette Children's Books

This Orchard
book belongs to

_____

_____

_____

Friday

Sunday

Wednesday

Saturday

Something Special

Nicola Moon

Illustrated by Alex Ayliffe

ORCHARD BOOKS

Friday was 'special' day in Mrs Brown's class. Everyone was allowed to bring in one of their favourite, special things to show the class.
"What can I take that's special?" asked Charlie one Friday morning. Mum was busy feeding Sally. "What about your teddy?" she said.

"Lots of people take their teddies," said Charlie.
"I want to take something different."
Sally started crying.
"Look in your bedroom," said Mum.

Charlie searched through his things.
There was Bessie, the old rag doll from
Africa that had belonged to his grandma.
But she didn't look very special with her
stuffing coming out.

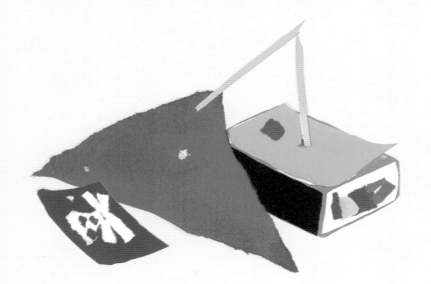

There was the model boat he'd made
all by himself. But it fell apart as soon
as he tried to pick it up.

There was the beautiful chocolate
rabbit he'd saved from Easter.
But one ear had been bitten off.

"I can't find anything," said Charlie sadly. "Can you help me look?"
Mum was busy dressing Sally.
"There's no time now," she said.
"Don't look so miserable. We can find something for next week."

When they got to school the other children had lots of special things.

Raju had some sweet and sticky gulab jamun that smelt of rose petals, and he let everyone taste them.

Peter had a strange looking plant called a 'Venus Fly Trap'. He said it ate flies and would eat your finger if you weren't careful.

Today is Friday

Lu Mei had a beautiful kite. It was made of bright red
paper and shaped like a dragon. She said it came from China.

Charlie's best friend Steven brought in his
pet hamster in a cage. Steven said its name was
Biscuit and Joanne said it looked like a rat.

And Daniel had a huge slimy worm
that he'd found on the way to school,
but Mrs Brown made him put it outside.

Shireen had a beautiful sari that sparkled blue and gold. She put it on and Mrs Brown said she looked like a princess.

But Charlie had nothing.
"Never mind," said Mrs Brown. "You can bring something to show us next week."

"But I haven't got anything special," said Charlie on his way home. "Not special and different."

"What about your favourite book? Or Goldie the fish? Or your collection of postcards from Uncle Ali in Nigeria?"

Mum tried hard to think of something.
"No, I don't want to take those," said Charlie.

When they got home Mum had to feed Sally again.
And change her nappy. And wash her clothes.
And put her to bed.

Charlie felt cross. He turned the television on really
loud. He stamped around and slammed the door.

"Ssh! You'll wake your sister," said Mum.

"I don't care!" said Charlie to himself.

Charlie felt Mum would never have time to help him find something special.

On Saturday they had to go to the shops in the rain, because Mum had to buy more nappies for Sally.

On Sunday Auntie Jill and Uncle John came, and they made a big fuss of Sally all day.

On Monday they were late for school because Sally had cried all night and they slept in.

On Tuesday Charlie went to Steven's house for tea. Steven had lots of special things. "You can borrow something if you like," he said.

"But it wouldn't be mine," said Charlie.

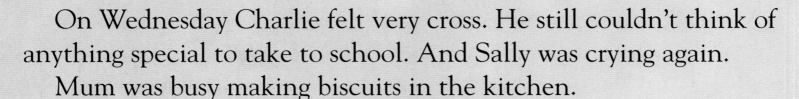

On Wednesday Charlie felt very cross. He still couldn't think of anything special to take to school. And Sally was crying again.

Mum was busy making biscuits in the kitchen.

"You go to her," she said.

"I don't want to." Charlie stamped his foot and started to cry. "All she does is cry all the time and I haven't got anything that's special, nothing at all."

Mum took Charlie onto her knee. "We'll find you something, you'll see. Now you go up and see Sally for me while I get the biscuits finished. Then you can have some warm from the oven, just how you like them."

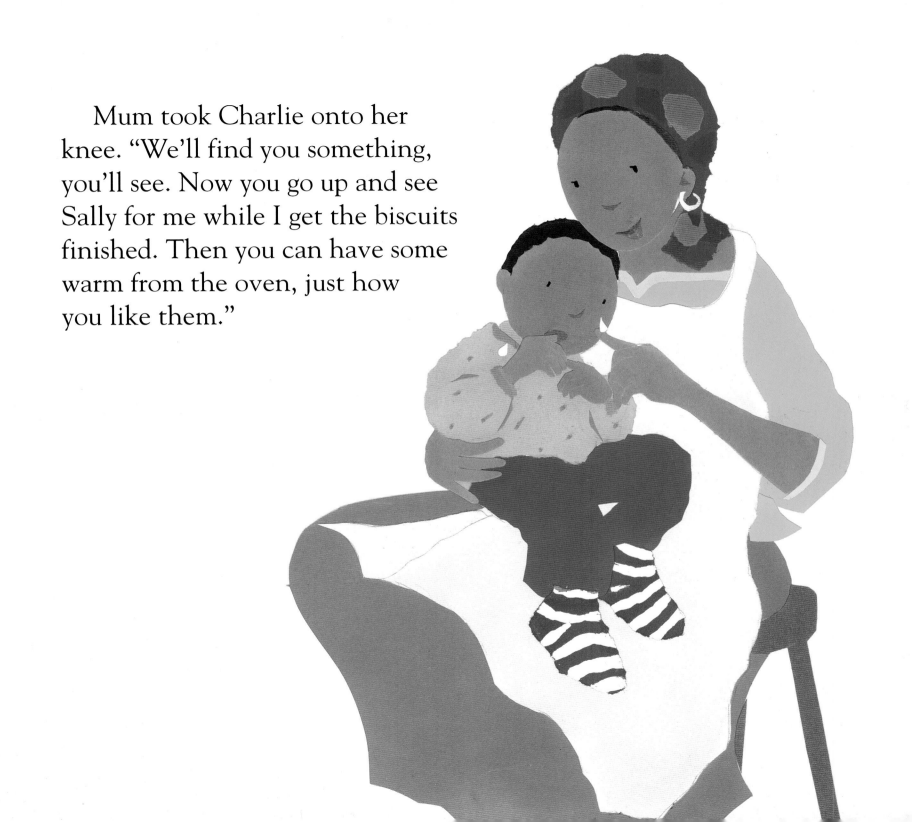

Charlie went slowly up the stairs and into Sally's room. He covered his ears and looked at his sister. Her face was all screwed up like an angry prune and she was kicking her legs wildly in the air.

"Stupid babies," he muttered. He picked up one of Sally's baby toys and started to play with it.

Sally stopped screaming. Charlie looked into the cot. Sally looked at Charlie with her big brown eyes. Charlie looked at Sally. Her hands were so tiny!

He reached out and touched her fingers. She grabbed
on to his finger so tightly he nearly cried out. But it felt nice.
He didn't know babies were so strong.

"Hello, Sally," he said. And then Sally
did something she'd never done before.
She smiled. A big beaming smile,
just for Charlie.

Later that evening Mum came to tuck Charlie into bed.
She held a wonderful carved wooden mask. "I've found
something for you to take to school," she said.
   "But I've already got something,"
said Charlie, and whispered in Mum's ear.

At school on Thursday Charlie was very excited.
"I'm bringing something really special tomorrow," he said.
"Is it a new toy?" asked Lu Mei.
"No," said Charlie.
"Is it your goldfish?" asked Steven.
"No," said Charlie.
"Is it something you can eat?" asked Daniel.
"No," said Charlie. "I'm not telling."

At last it was Friday. The other children were already waiting when Mum brought Charlie into the classroom.

"Charlie has something special to show us this morning," said Mrs Brown.

Today is Friday

"This is my baby sister," said Charlie proudly.
"She's called Sally and she's six weeks old and
she smiles at me and she's very, very special."

"She looks like you," said Peter.

"When will she be big enough to
play football?" said Daniel.

"You are lucky," said Joanne.
"I wish I had a baby sister," said Lu Mei.
"She isn't smiling at me," said Steven.
"She only smiles at me," said Charlie,
"because I'm her brother."

That night Charlie helped Mum to bath
Sally and put her to bed.
"Do you know what special day it will be
tomorrow?" asked Mum, when Sally was asleep.
"No," said Charlie.

"It's going to be 'big brother day'," said Mum.
"A special day for big brothers, because big
brothers really are 'something special'."

Friday

Sunday

Wednesday

Saturday